MOBILE SERVICES

JAN BRETT'S ANIMAL TREASURY

G. P. PUTNAM'S SONS

G. P. PUTNAM'S SONS

an imprint of Penguin Random House LLC

375 Hudson Street

New York, NY 10014

Jan Brett's Animal Treasury copyright © 2017 by Jan Brett.

Town Mouse, Country Mouse copyright © 1994 by Jan Brett.

Armadillo Rodeo copyright © 1995 by Jan Brett.

The Umbrella copyright © 2004 by Jan Brett.

The Three Snow Bears copyright © 2007 by Jan Brett.

G. P. Putnam's Sons is a registered trademark of Penguin Random House LLC.

Library of Congress Cataloging-in-Publication Data is available upon request.

Manufactured in China by RR Donnelley Asia Printing Solutions Ltd.

ISBN 9781524738020

1 3 5 7 9 10 8 6 4 2

Aworld of animals awaited me in the big gray barn behind my childhood home. The donkey, horse, guinea pigs, and chickens all seemed to have stories to tell.

One day, exploring the hayloft, my sisters and I found an animal's nest. Inside was a small lusterware pitcher, scraps of velvet, and a golden ring. We were sure it was the house of the Town Mouse from Aesop's fable.

Researching for my children's books led to more exploration. When I visited a polar bear at the Brookfield Zoo in Chicago, I saw his gray tongue and patted his fur (he was anesthetized for a medical exam). A curious armadillo that looked like a walking cowboy boot led me on a merry chase through Texas, and a trip to Costa Rica revealed the enchanting wildlife of the rain forest.

Animals have been imagined in the parts in tales told in cultures around the world. Their stories unfold in the land between real and make-believe, a place I would like to take you to in the stories in this book.

Jan Brett

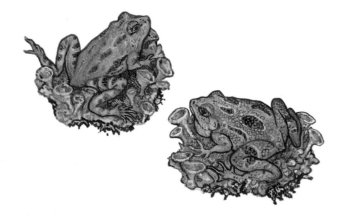

JAN BRETT

TOWN MOUSE

COUNTRY MOUSE

For my niece,
Sophie Tsairis

TOWN MOUSE
COUNTRY MOUSE

One morning, the town mouse woke up shivering from a dream about the kitchen cat who prowled the house. "I need a vacation," he said to his wife. "Let me take you to see the countryside where I was born. Life is quiet and peaceful there. The sun shines brightly every day, and the air is so clear that you can see the stars at night. And nothing will prepare you for the taste of wild blackberries." "Let's go right away!" she said. So the town mouse and his wife packed a picnic and set off for the country.

The country mouse and her husband were at their tree-stump house, exhausted from searching for food and avoiding the hungry owl who lived nearby. "Sometimes I wish we lived in a town house where all the food you can eat is right there in the pantry. They say that the smell of cheese makes your whiskers tingle." "Mine are tingling already," her husband exclaimed.

The town mice were outside the country mice's house putting a huge chunk of cheese in the middle of their picnic cloth. The country mice peered down at it. They heard the town mouse exclaim: "This is the life! Wildflowers, spring peepers. If only we lived here!" The country mice crept out. "You like it here?" they asked. "Why, we've always wanted to live in a town house." The town mouse offered them a nibble of cheese. "Why don't we trade houses?" he said. "Would you?" asked the country mouse, her mouth stuffed full of the delicious cheese. "We'll leave right away," she said. As they said good-bye, each of the mice thought that they had the better part of the bargain.

It was dark when the country mice arrived in town and found the house. They tiptoed inside and wandered into the sewing room where they found what they thought was a sumptuous bed and fell sound asleep. Much too early the next morning, a loud clanging woke them up. Sooty clouds of smoke were pouring over them and they heard a strange voice purring loudly: "Sauces and ham, it's hungry I am! Sauces and ham, it's hungry I am. Mice in my stew, wait till I catch you!" "Who do you think *that* is?" the country mouse asked his wife.

The town mouse and his wife were up with the birds, ready to gather wild blackberries in the grassy meadow for breakfast. They could smell them. They just couldn't find them. As the town mouse's wife turned to remind her husband to remember the way home, she felt a large wet drop on her head. "What was that?" she asked. "Is the bathtub leaking?" "No, we're in the country now," he said. "Those are raindrops." Just then, lightning lit up the sky, and rain poured down as the two drenched mice ran wildly for their tree-stump home.

The country mice were looking forward to their first splendid meal in the pantry. "I'm sure there is ham in the ice chest and rolls in the bread box. But the best smell of all is coming from up there," the country mouse told her husband. "It must be a fine old cheese. I'll climb on your shoulders and get it." But she couldn't quite reach it. "Stand on your toes," she called down. But just as she got ahold of the cheese, her husband lost his balance. The top slammed down, and she was left hanging by her tail. "Help me! Help me! I'm caught."

Back in the country, the town mouse had put on dry clothes. He was especially proud of his bright new jacket. "So colorful and eye-catching," he said to his wife. "Let's stroll in the forest. We'll come back loaded with acorns and hickory nuts." But their walk was soon interrupted. The town mouse's colorful coat was so eye-catching that it caught the eye of a curious black bird, and if his wife hadn't held him by his foot, he would have been carried off.

Not far away in town, the country mouse felt his wife's silky tail. "Nothing broken," he said. But when he looked in her eyes, he saw how sad and discouraged she was. "I know something that will cheer us up," he told her. "Follow me." He had spied a small window up above the pantry shelves. Together they climbed higher and higher. When they reached the top, he rubbed away the soot, and they looked out at a piece of blue sky. "Doesn't it look like home?" the country mouse asked his wife.

The town mice stood quietly together after their awful black bird scare. "I thought I had lost you forever," the town mouse whispered to her husband. They looked around. How still and peaceful it was now. The sun had come out, and everything was glistening and green. "It is beautiful here," she said. "We should try to enjoy it." "I know," the town mouse said. "But I miss the sound of the town—all the hustle and bustle. Here I feel so alone." "And in our cozy town house, we knew what to expect," his wife added.

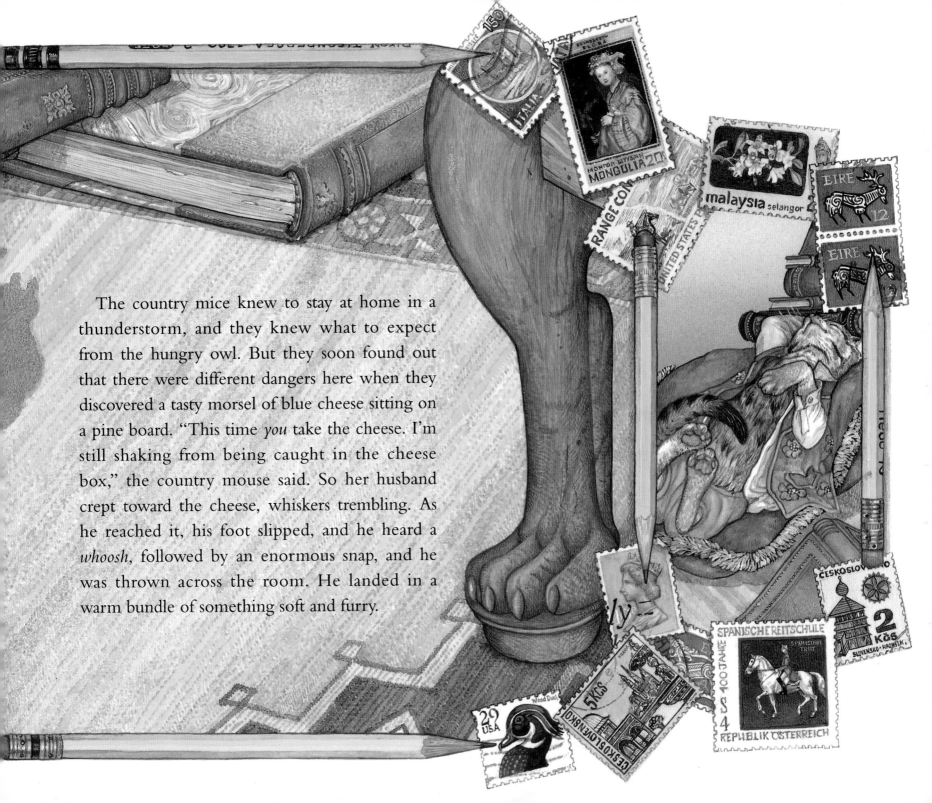

The country mice knew to stay at home in a thunderstorm, and they knew what to expect from the hungry owl. But they soon found out that there were different dangers here when they discovered a tasty morsel of blue cheese sitting on a pine board. "This time *you* take the cheese. I'm still shaking from being caught in the cheese box," the country mouse said. So her husband crept toward the cheese, whiskers trembling. As he reached it, his foot slipped, and he heard a *whoosh*, followed by an enormous snap, and he was thrown across the room. He landed in a warm bundle of something soft and furry.

The country mouse was shaking from his close call. "I can barely stand." He winced as his wife pulled him up and patted down his crumpled whiskers. It was then that she noticed the bundle on which her husband had landed was tipping and turning. It was alive! Two green eyes snapped open. "Run!" she cried, getting a good look at it. "It's an owl with teeth!"

The town mice knew how to avoid mousetraps set with cheese, but they soon found that the country has its own perils when they explored the riverbank, hand in hand. Suddenly the water began to boil and churn and a huge wet head popped up and stared at them. It was a river otter. The mice tore back to their tree-stump home, only to find a hedgehog rolled into a ball in front of the door. Then they heard an animal crashing toward them through the underbrush. "I can't take this anymore!" the town mouse quaked, and she raced for the nearest tree with her husband right behind her.

From the tree, they could see the town lights blink on as the sun went down and the stars came out one by one. "What shall we do?" the town mouse asked his wife. But before she could answer, she saw a pair of glowering eyes right beside them and they were face to face with the most terrifying creature of all. "A cat with wings!" shrieked the town mouse. "That's it for me!" his wife cried, and they ran down the tree and toward the town as fast as their legs could take them.

As the town mice headed frantically along the road, the country mice were fleeing in terror toward the country. Their paths crossed, but neither saw the other, they were so frightened. Even the sky seemed to be falling down on them! The country mice didn't stop running until they could see their tree stump in the distance.

The town mice kept on running until they reached their town house. The musty smell of old wood, and smoke from the kitchen, all seemed wonderful. Even the street sounds outside sounded cheerful and friendly. "There's no place like home," sighed the town mouse, as he and his wife settled into a warm old slipper. "There's no place like home."

Atop their cozy tree-stump house, the country mouse and her husband looked up at a full moon shining down on them. They sighed happily. "We missed you," they said together.

Back on the road, the cat and owl had knocked each other out when they collided head-on. The cat, slowly waking up, touched his bruised head gingerly. He looked up to see the owl brushing himself off. It was then that he had an idea. "Owl, how would you like to trade places with me? I've always wanted to try the simple life in the country!"

For Jason Merrill

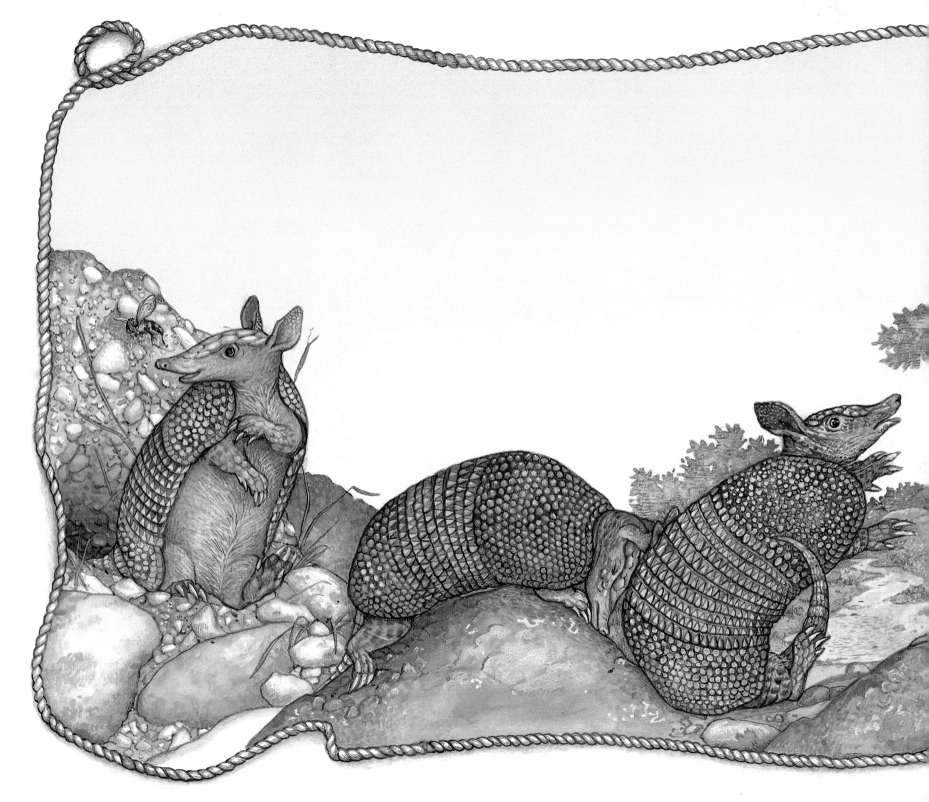

Armadillos, one, two, three—Bo! Let's go," Ma Armadillo called to her boys as they headed out to dig, deep in the heart of Texas hill country.

"Stay close!" Her boys didn't see too well, just like all armadillos, and she didn't want to lose them, especially Bo, who was always wandering off.

"One, two, three—Bo! Don't go gettin' distracted on me." But Bo already was. He was looking at a lizard.

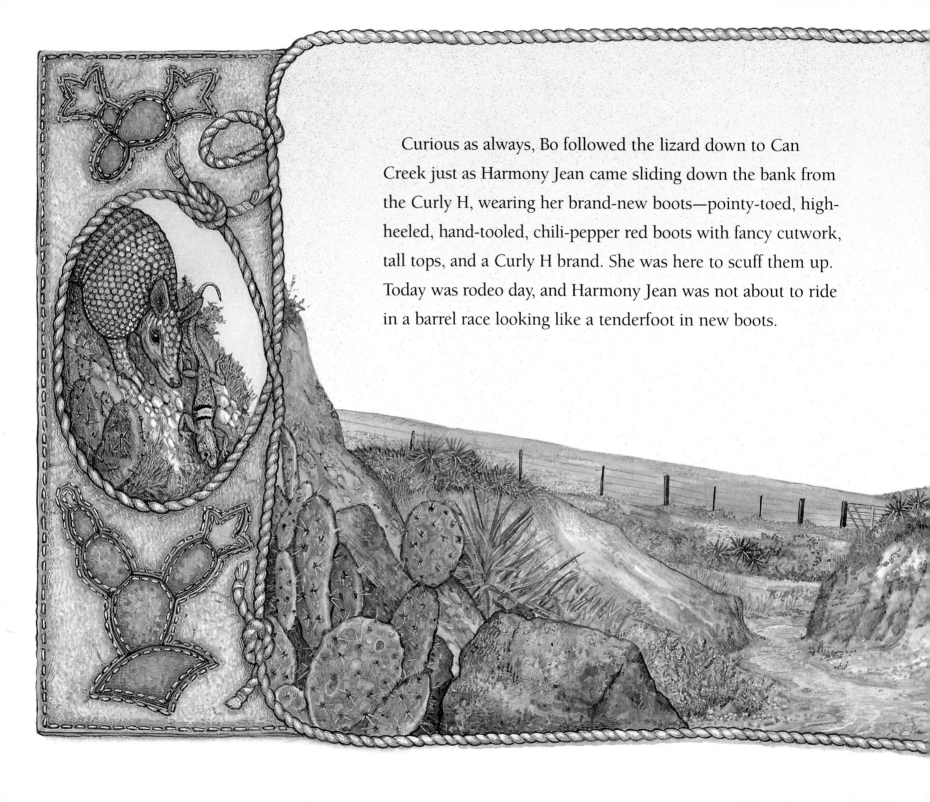

Curious as always, Bo followed the lizard down to Can Creek just as Harmony Jean came sliding down the bank from the Curly H, wearing her brand-new boots—pointy-toed, high-heeled, hand-tooled, chili-pepper red boots with fancy cutwork, tall tops, and a Curly H brand. She was here to scuff them up. Today was rodeo day, and Harmony Jean was not about to ride in a barrel race looking like a tenderfoot in new boots.

She found a muddy place and hopped and splashed until her boots had a worn, lived-in look. Pleased, she whooped and hollered, "Look at me! Won't you just look at me!"

Bo's ears perked up at the sound of that pretty voice. He lifted his head and squinted. What he saw was all that red leather shimmering and prancing over the creek bed. Why, for sure, it looked to Bo as if he'd found a friend, a rip-roarin', rootin'-tootin', shiny red armadillo! Bo grinned. "Howdy!" he shouted.

Harmony Jean, job done, lit off through the back forty to the Curly H. Bo never looked back. He blinked and squinted as he trundled after his bright red friend as fast as he could go. "Wait up!" he called.

Back at the creek, his mama twitched an ear. "Is that hollerin' one of my boys?" she asked.

"Armadillos! One, two, three—Oh no, Bo!" He'd done it again.

Bo arrived at the rodeo just as Harmony Jean was swinging a leg up on her pony, Spotlight. He saw the perky nose and silvery tail of the red armadillo leaping up ahead of him.

"Wait for me!" Bo called.

When Spotlight felt Bo on his back, he gave a hopping buck. Harmony Jean stayed aboard, but Bo was tossed high in the air.

The little armadillo landed in the dust. As he unrolled, he smiled, brushed himself off, and shouted, "Hey, pardner! You're my kind of friend!"

Bo tried to catch sight of that rootin'-tootin' red armadillo, but he had to move fast. As he zigged and zagged across the arena, Ma Armadillo, with her three boys, was hot on his trail, asking everyone she met if they'd seen her Bo.

Bo was still looking when he saw the armadillo headed for the Bar-B-Q. "I'm right behind you," Bo called.

But before he could catch up, the armadillo disappeared
under the blue-checked tablecloth. Bo dove after him and
peered around. His friend was nibbling on something green, so
Bo ambled over and took a big bite. It was a red-hot, bright-green
jalapeño pepper.

His mouth on fire, Bo ran out and doused his head in lemon-
ade to stop the burn. "Delicious," he gulped. "What's next?"

Chow time over, the cowhands got out their fiddles and everyone went into the barn for a little dancing. Bo struggled to see his pal. Finally he spotted a flash of red, right in the middle of all those stomping feet. Bo two-stepped toward his frisky new friend and cut in.

Harmony Jean went tap-slide-tap with her right foot, then heel-stomped, high-kicked with her left, and Bo was hurled high in the air. As he landed in the hayloft, he let out a rebel yell: "Yaaa-Hoo!"

Not far away, Ma Armadillo heard the commotion. "That's my Bo," she cried.

By the time Bo made it down the hay chute, the dance floor was empty. Harmony Jean and her friends had settled around the campfire. She looked down at her boots. They were starting to pinch. She slipped them off and tossed them behind her.

Bo bounded up to a pointy-toed, high-heeled, hand-tooled, chili-pepper red boot. "Howdy," he said. "You're a mighty hard fellow to keep up with. My name's Bo. What's yours?" His new friend didn't answer.

Bo stepped even closer. He could see the perky nose and the shy smile. "What's next?" he asked.

But instead of answering, his friend fell over, *plop,* and Bo was left looking down an opening. He stuck his head in and sniffed. It didn't smell like an armadillo. He poked his nose against the leather. It didn't feel like an armadillo. He squinted up close. It didn't even look like an armadillo. Nose in the air, he wailed, "You're not an armadilloooooooo!"

Not far away, the sharp ears of his ma recognized the voice of her boy. His three brothers heard him too. Their search was over. "Boys, let's go get Bo and head on home."

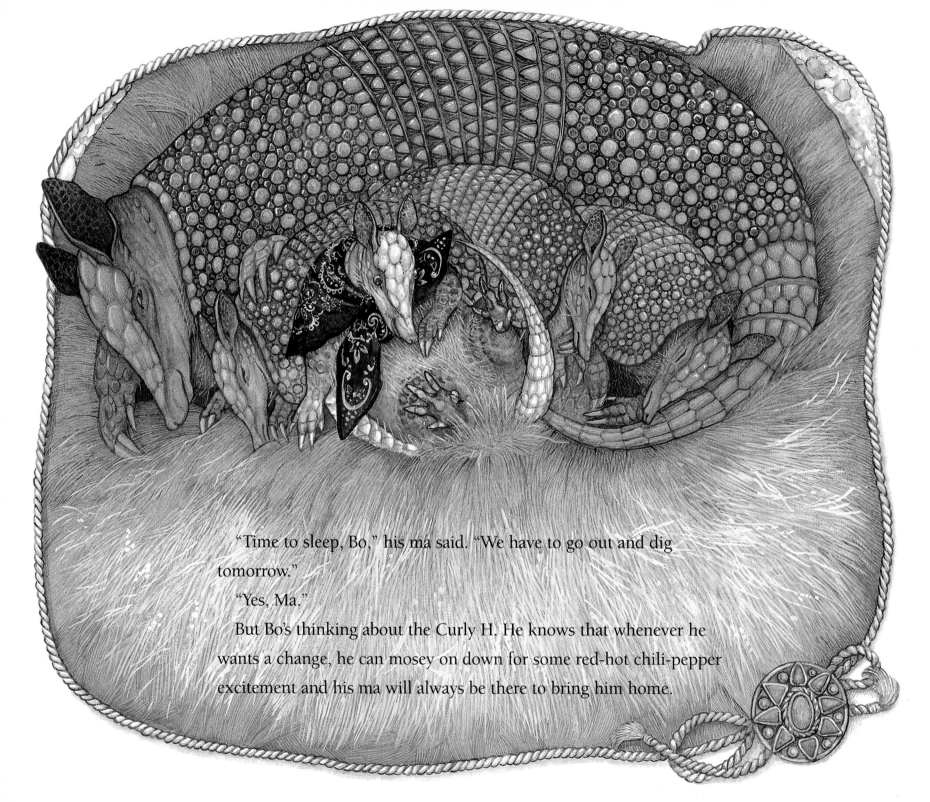

"Time to sleep, Bo," his ma said. "We have to go out and dig
tomorrow."

"Yes, Ma."

But Bo's thinking about the Curly H. He knows that whenever he
wants a change, he can mosey on down for some red-hot chili-pepper
excitement and his ma will always be there to bring him home.

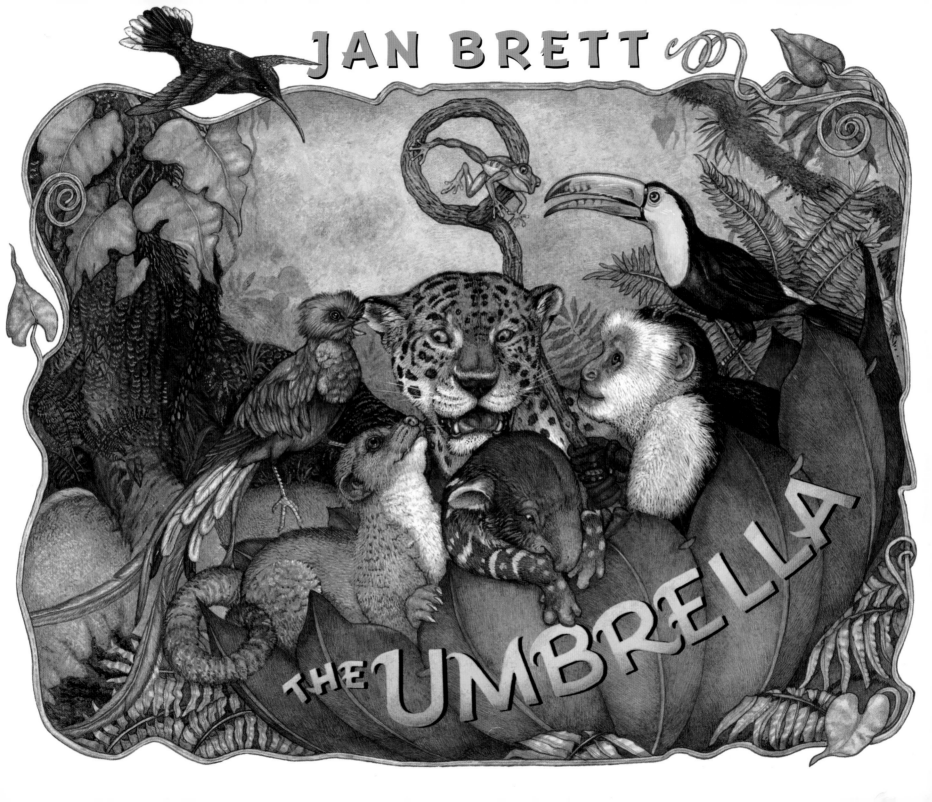

JAN BRETT

THE UMBRELLA

For
Bethany
Susana
Fusiek

With special thanks to
Nicole Brocco and Lois Ostapczuk

"Hey, little Carlos, where are you going with that umbrella?"

"Into the cloud forest, Papa, to see what I can see. I'll be spotting a jaguar and a monkey. For sure I'll spy a toucan and a kinkajou. I'll keep my eyes peeled for a shy tapir."

"*Buena suerte,* Carlos, good luck," Papa says.

Carlos walks into the cloud forest. How silent it is. The only sound is the drip, drip, drip of drops falling from the tall trees.

There's not so much as a tiny tree frog down here, Carlos thinks. I'll have to climb up for a better view.

Carlos drops his umbrella and starts up the giant fig tree.

Drip, drip, drip. A little puddle appears in the green umbrella.

A tiny tree frog leaps down and slips into the water. *"Hola,"* Froggy croaks happily. "I have this puddle all to myself." He sinks down until only his eyes peep out.

Plop! A juicy, ripe fig falls smack into the umbrella. Toucan is not far behind.

Froggy sees Toucan's sharp beak. *"¡Vete!"* he peeps. "Go away!" But Toucan is not moving, he's waiting for another fig to fall.

High in the tree, a scratching sound starts. Scratch . . .
scratch . . . SCRATCH! Something is sliding down the tree.
It gets louder and louder until THUMP — Kinkajou tumbles in.

"*¡Muy grande!*" Froggy squeaks. "You're too big!"

"You can't stay here!" Toucan says.

But Kinkajou is just getting comfortable. After prowling
around all night for food, he's found just the right place to rest.

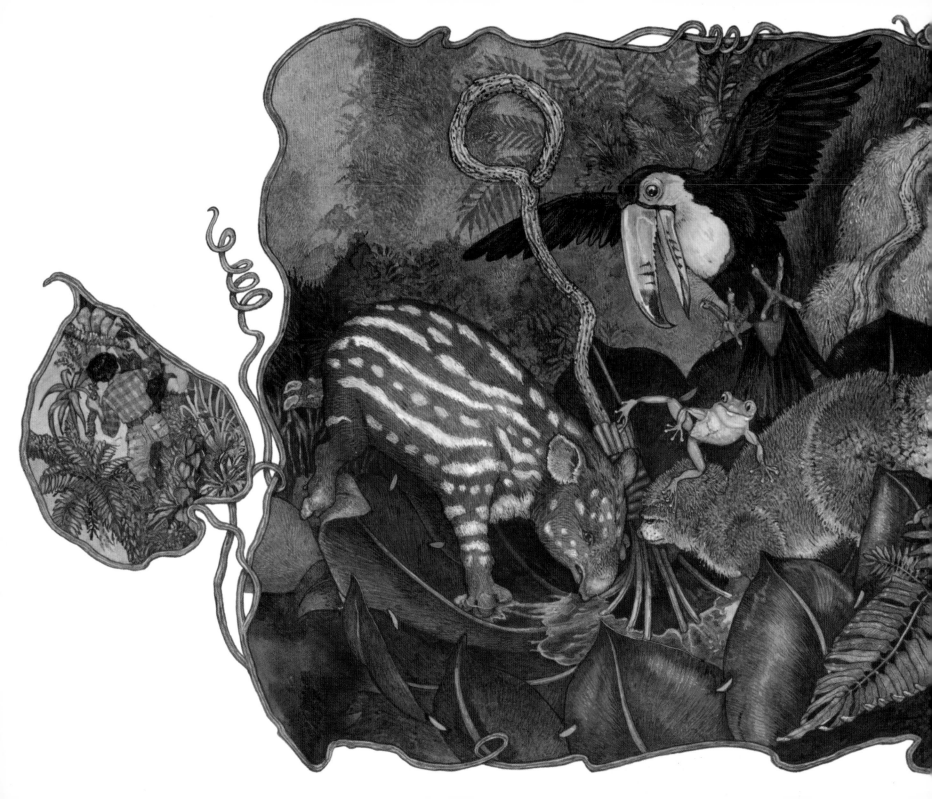

Thump! Crash! Thump! Baby Tapir blunders into the green umbrella. "Blaaht, blaaaaaaht!" he bawls. "Mama!"

"*¡No está aquí!* She's not here!" Froggy shouts, along with hungry Toucan and sleepy Kinkajou.

The umbrella's shiny green leaves shiver and shake, but Baby Tapir is staying here until his mother comes for him.

Swish! Swish! A most beautiful bird sails down onto the umbrella handle. Quetzal looks down at Froggy, Toucan, Kinkajou and Baby Tapir, rocking back and forth.

"Fly away," they call up. But proud Quetzal is too busy arranging his tail plumes to listen to them.

Suddenly, frisky Monkey jumps down. He grabs the umbrella, flings it into the river and jumps aboard.

"*¿Qué pasa?* What is happening?" Froggy asks as water starts to pour into the umbrella.

"We will sink for sure!" Toucan, Kinkajou, Baby Tapir and Quetzal wail together. "That Monkey never thinks before he acts."

"¡Atención! Who's sitting on me?" Froggy cries.

"Stop poking your beak into me," Kinkajou shouts at Toucan.

"Blaaht!" bawls Baby Tapir.

"You're getting my feathers all wet," Quetzal squawks at Monkey.

Jaguar is cleaning his silky black spots when he hears all the squabbling and looks up.

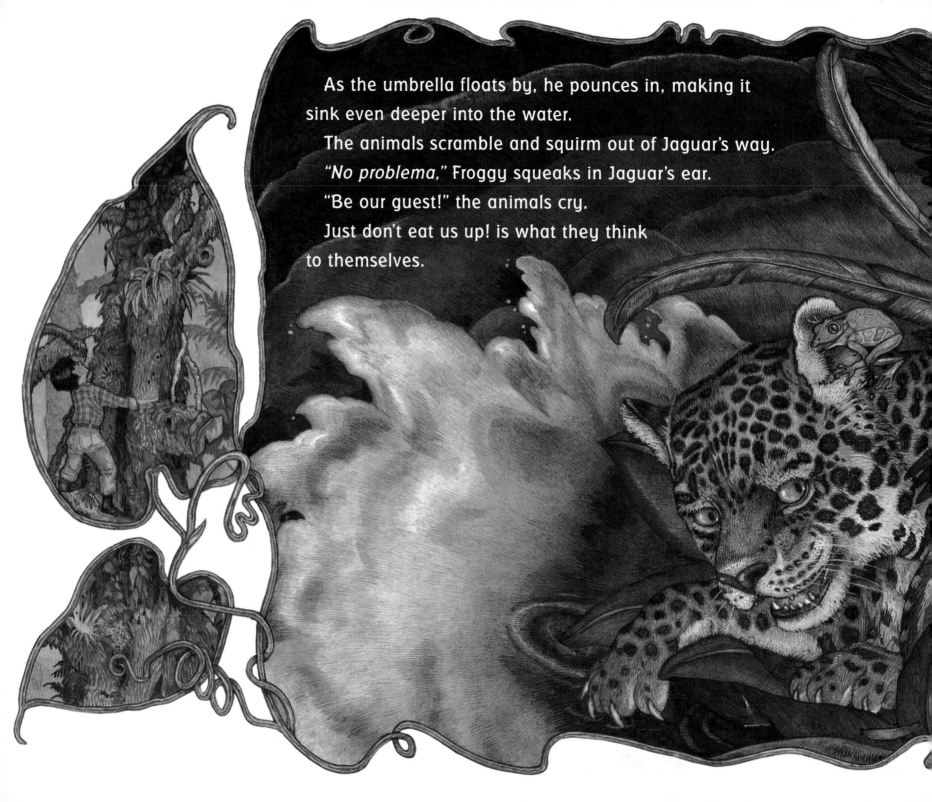

As the umbrella floats by, he pounces in, making it
sink even deeper into the water.

The animals scramble and squirm out of Jaguar's way.

"No problema," Froggy squeaks in Jaguar's ear.

"Be our guest!" the animals cry.

Just don't eat us up! is what they think
to themselves.

Hummingbird flashes by, smaller than small.
He sees the big green umbrella handle sticking up,
just the place for a hummingbird to stop for a little rest.
   As he is about to land, they all start shouting.
   "No room," big boy Jaguar snarls.
   "Move on," Monkey hollers.
   "Find another place," Quetzal sings out.
   "We got here first," Kinkajou growls.
   "Stay away," Toucan screeches.
   "Blaaaht," bawls Baby Tapir.
   "*¡Adiós!* Good-bye!" Froggy peeps.
   But Hummingbird lands anyway.

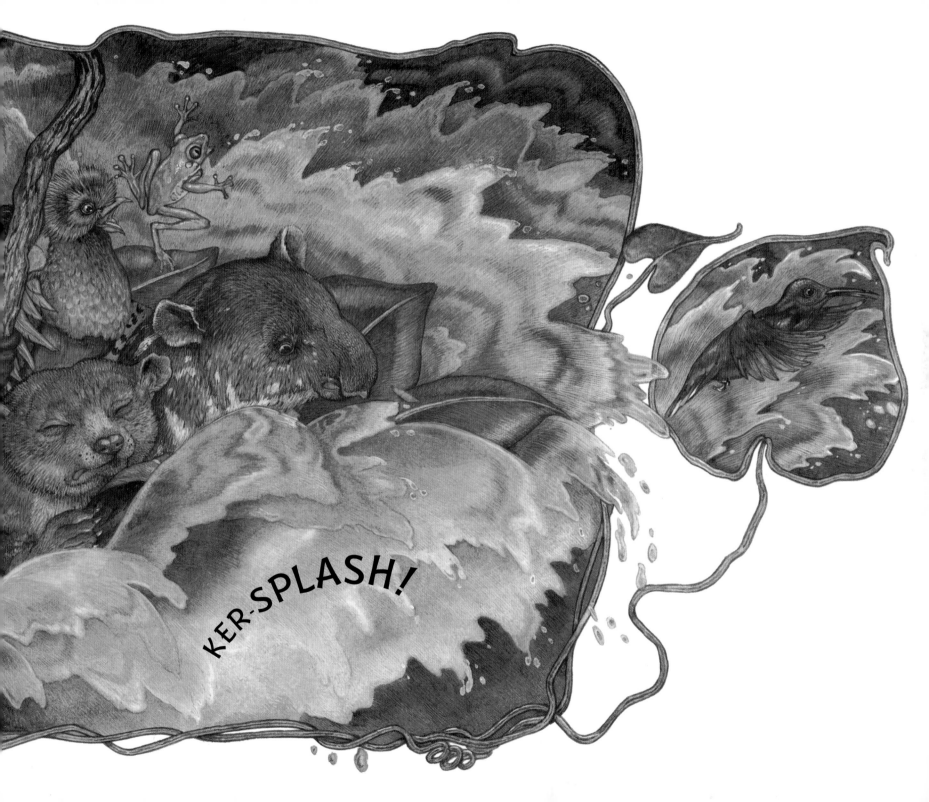

KER-SPLASH!

The umbrella tumbles over, and everyone falls out.
Jaguar, Quetzal, Baby Tapir, Kinkajou, Toucan, Monkey
and Froggy all clamber up the bank as the umbrella pops
to the surface and drifts back to shore.

Up in the giant fig tree, Carlos looks out at the sea of green.
"No animals today," he sighs. "I wonder where they all are."
He climbs down, picks up his umbrella and walks toward home.

The sun shines through the green leaves of the umbrella, and Carlos sees the silhouette of the tiny tree frog.

"Hey, little froggy, try hitchhiking with me tomorrow, and I'll show you a real adventure. I'm going back to the cloud forest to find a toucan, a kinkajou, maybe even a monkey or a shy tapir. I bet I'll see a jaguar too. And I'm going to find that quetzal for sure."

Carlos props the umbrella outside his door.
Drip, drip, drip. Water falls from the roof. A little
puddle appears in the green umbrella. Froggy slides
down the handle and slips into the water.

"*¡Hola!*" Froggy splashes happily. "I have
this puddle all to myself."

For Katie

With thanks to the Brookfield Zoo

THE THREE SNOW BEARS

Come back!" Aloo-ki shouted as her huskies floated out to sea. *Oh, no!* She knew that although an ice floe is a good place to fish, it is a bad place to lose a dog team.

Not far away a snow bear family had just started to eat their breakfast. But it was way too hot for Baby Bear.

"Ow-ee!" yowled Baby Bear. "My breakfast burned my mouth."

"We'll go for a stroll and let the soup cool," Mama Bear said.

Aloo-ki was running along looking for her dogs when she came upon the biggest igloo she had ever seen.

Who lives here? she wondered.

Aloo-ki ducked inside. Right away, she smelled something delicious.

Across the room, she saw a big bowl, a middle-sized bowl, and a small bowl. Surely the good smell was coming from the three bowls.

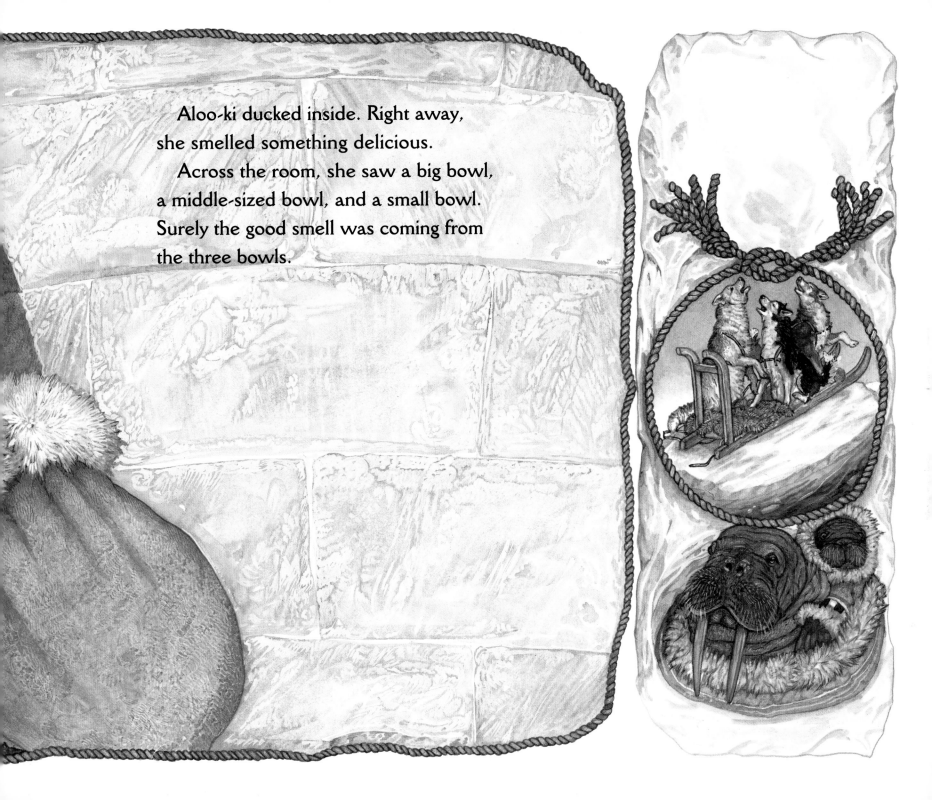

Aloo-ki took a sip from the biggest bowl.
"Owwwwww!" she cried out. "Too hot!"
She took a sip from the middle-sized bowl.
"Ewwwwww! Too cold!"
She tipped up the littlest bowl and drank every drop.
"Mmmmmm!" she said. "Not too hot and not too cold."

In the next room Aloo-ki spotted three pairs of beautiful boots standing in a row.

She put on the biggest boot. "Too big!" she said.

She put on the middle-sized boot. "Too fancy!" she said.

She put on the littlest pair. "Just right!" she said, wiggling her toes in the soft fur lining.

Aloo-ki walked into the last room and found a long
sleeping bench piled high with fur covers. Heat from
an oil lamp warmed her cheeks and made her sleepy.
Time for a nap, she thought.

She crawled under the highest mound of covers.
"Too lumpy," she grumbled. She tried the middle bed
with the furry fringe cover, but sank down so far
that she could hardly breathe. "Too soft," she said.

She rolled over into the smallest
sleeping place. The furry blanket
was cozy and warm and the pillow
was just her size.

"Just right," Aloo-ki murmured
and was asleep before she
could take her boots off.

If Aloo-ki hadn't fallen fast asleep,
she might have heard her dogs
barking happily.

Papa Bear, Mama Bear, and Baby Bear
had spotted them adrift in the strong current
and gone out to save them. The snow bear
family was pushing Aloo-ki's dog team back
toward their igloo and safety.

Papa Bear crawled into the igloo and saw his big bowl sitting in a pool of spilled soup. "Someone has been tasting my soup!" he roared.

Mama Bear rushed in and saw that her soup had been sloshed around too. "Someone has been sipping my soup," she growled.

"Someone found my soup!" sputtered Baby Bear in her high, squeaky voice. "And they ate it all up!"

Papa Bear ran into the next room and saw his boots in the middle of the floor. "Someone has been trying on my boots," he boomed in his big bear voice.

Mama Bear put on her fancy boots. "Someone has had these boots on," she huffed, "and the fur is all bunched up."

Baby Bear saw that her boots had disappeared. "Someone has taken my boots and left behind these not as good ones!" she wailed.

The bears ran into
their bedroom.

"Someone has been sleeping in my bed!" Papa Bear
bellowed.

"Someone has been sleeping in my bed too!"
Mama Bear cried.

Baby Bear peeked at her little bed and squeaked,
"Someone has been sleeping in my bed, and here she is!"

Aloo-ki opened her eyes and saw
three bear noses only inches away.

She hopped out of bed and
dove between Papa Bear's
huge furry LEGS!

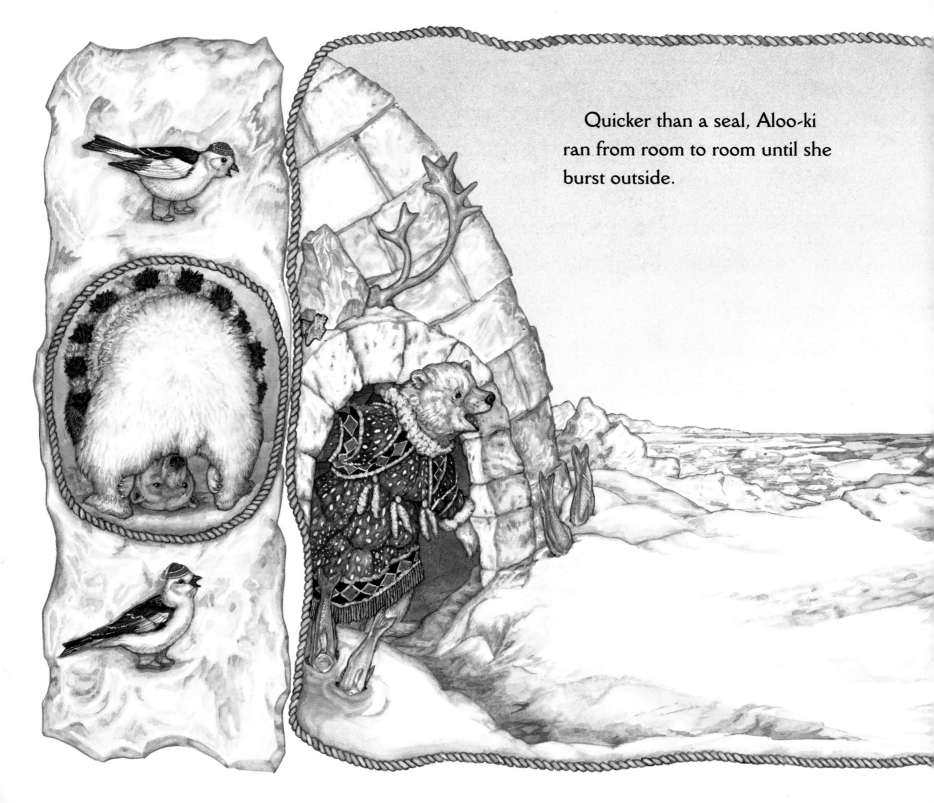

Quicker than a seal, Aloo-ki
ran from room to room until she
burst outside.

Her huskies bounced around, barking
and smiling their doggy grins.

Aloo-ki and her dogs flew over the frozen ice,
dodging ridges and cracks. She looked back
to wave a thank-you to the snow bears.

She couldn't see them, but she heard a big gruff voice, a middle-sized voice, and a high, squeaky voice calling to her . . .